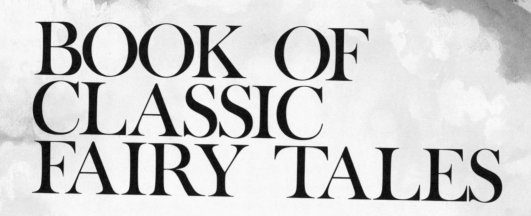

BOOK OF CLASSIC FAIRY TALES

Three Billy-Goats Gruff   6
Little Red Hen   11
Sleeping Beauty   14
Hansel and Gretel   21
Chicken Licken   25
Twelve Dancing Princesses   28
The Princess and the Pea   34
The Three Little Pigs   36
Little Red Riding Hood   41
Puss in Boots   46
The Ugly Duckling   51
Rumpelstiltskin   55

Illustrated by Eric Kincaid, Gerry Embleton
and Gill Embleton

BRIMAX BOOKS · NEWMARKET · ENGLAND

The Three Billy-Goats Gruff

Once upon a time and far, far away in a land of beautiful mountains, fine green fields and sparkling streams, there lived three billy-goats. They were all named Gruff.

The eldest and largest was called Big Billy-Goat Gruff; the next was called Middle Billy-Goat Gruff; and the youngest and smallest was called Tiny Billy-Goat Gruff.

They had eaten all the grass in their field; they were hungry and getting thinner every day. So, they set off to find a better place, where they could eat and grow fat.

In the distance, on the other side of a wide stream, they saw a fine green field. The grass was thick and long; it was just what they wanted.

"We would get fat on that," said Tiny Billy-Goat Gruff in his little voice.

"Oh yes, we would," added Middle Billy-Goat Gruff in his soft voice.

"Then we must go at once," said Big Billy-Goat Gruff in his loud voice.

Over the stream was a wooden bridge to be crossed and under the bridge lived a troll. Now, a troll is a bad-tempered, ugly dwarf, who has big eyes and a long nose. He likes nothing better than eating goat for his supper. The children who lived in a village nearby, stayed well away from the wooden bridge. Everyone was afraid of the ugly troll.

The three billy-goats looked at the bridge.

"What about the Troll?" asked Tiny Billy-Goat Gruff in his little voice.

"Yes, what about the Troll?" added Middle Billy-Goat Gruff in his soft voice.

"I have a plan," declared Big Billy-Goat Gruff in his loud voice. "Listen carefully." The three goats put their heads close together and they whispered to one another.

Tiny Billy-Goat Gruff was the first to reach the bridge. Trip, trip, trip . . . went his tiny hooves on the wooden boards.

Out came the ugly Troll.

"Who is that?" he roared. "Who is that tripping over my bridge?"

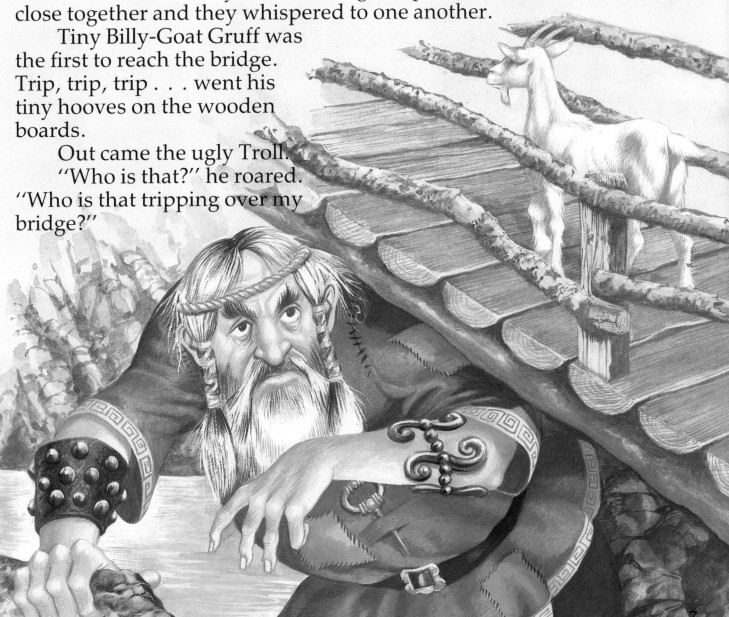

"Oh!" cried Tiny Billy-Goat Gruff in his little voice. "I am Tiny, the smallest Billy-Goat Gruff. I am going to that field over there to eat and grow fat."

"Ha!" roared the Troll again. "No, you are not! I am going to eat YOU!"

Poor Tiny Goat began to shak He trembled all over.

"Oh, no! Do not bother with me . . . I am very small and I am s thin. Why not wait for the next Billy-Goat Gruff, he is much bigge and fatter."

The ugly Troll stopped to think.

"Very well!" he shouted. "Be off with you!"

So Tiny Billy-Goat Gruff quickly tripped over the bridge and into the fine green field.

Before long, up came Middle Billy-Goat Gruff. Trip, trot, trip, trot . . . went his hooves on the wooden boards.

Out came the ugly Troll.

"Who is that?" he roared. "Who is that trotting over my bridge?"

"Oh!" cried Middle Billy-Goat Gruff in his soft voice. "I am Middle, the second Billy-Goat Gruff. I am on my way to the field over there to eat and grow fat."

"Ha!" roared the Troll again. "No, you are not! I am going to eat YOU!"

Poor Middle Goat began to shake. He trembled all over.

"Oh, no! Do not bother with me . . . I am middle-sized and really quite thin. Why not wait for Big Billy-Goat Gruff; he is really big and very much fatter."

The ugly Troll stopped to think.

"Very well!" he shouted. "Be off with you!"

So Middle Billy-Goat Gruff quickly trotted over the bridge and into the fine green field.

Then came Big Billy-Goat Gruff. Trip, trot, tramp! Trip, trot, tramp . . . went his big hooves on the wooden boards.

Out came the ugly Troll.

"Who is that?" he roared louder than ever. "Who is that tramping over my bridge?"

"Ah!" replied Big Billy-Goat Gruff in his loudest voice. "I am Big, the biggest Billy-Goat Gruff . . . and I am tramping over this bridge!"

The ugly Troll roared with anger. "I am coming to get you," he shouted. He moved a few steps towards the goat.

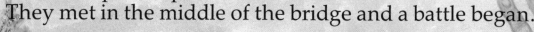

"Oh, no, you are not!" bellowed Big Billy-Goat Gruff. "I am coming to get YOU!"

He lowered his head and stamped his hooves. Tramp, tramp, TRAMP! Tramp, tramp, TRAMP!

They met in the middle of the bridge and a battle began.

Big Billy-Goat Gruff prodded the ugly Troll with his sharp horns. He picked him up and tossed him into the air. The ugly Troll turned three somersaults before he fell with a splash into the deep water of the stream. He was never seen again.

So Big Billy-Goat Gruff tramped happily across the bridge and into the fine green field. All three billy-goats ate the sweet grass and grew fatter and fatter.

The children in the village were happy. They could use the bridge and play in the fields, for the ugly old Troll was gone forever.

Little Red Hen

Little Red Hen strutted out of the farmyard and into Farmer Brown's big field. The wheat had been cut and gathered so she could scratch about anywhere.

"I might find some ears of wheat that the farmer's men have dropped," she clucked.

And she did. They were fine fat ones, full of golden grains. She carried them back to the farmyard to show her friends.

"Cluck, cluck!" called Little Red Hen. "Will you help me plant these grains?"

"Oh, No-o-!" yawned Ginger Cat. "I'm too sleee-py." Ginger Cat went up onto the roof of the barn and went to sleep.

"Oh, No-o-!" squeaked Grey Rat. "I am busy storing winter food in the barn." Grey Rat scampered away.

"Oh, No-o!" grunted Pink Pig. "I am off to find some acorns." She trotted away into the trees.

"Very well," said Little Red Hen. "I will plant them myself."

And she did. She put them in fine straight rows. She watched the rows every day. She saw green shoots peeping up out of the ground. Then she saw the wheat at the top begin to ripen in the sunshine. Little Red Hen was pleased.

"My wheat is ready!" called Little Red Hen to the animals. "Will you help me gather it?"

"Not today," said Ginger Cat. "I must wash my fur."

"Don't count on me," squeaked Grey Rat. "My work is never done."

"You can see I'm too busy," grunted Pink Pig. "I have ten piglets to feed!"

"Very well," said Little Red Hen. "I will gather it myself."

And she did. She snipped each stalk and made a neat bundle.

"That's done!" she clucked. "Will you help me carry the wheat to the miller? The miller will grind it into flour."

"Impossible!" said Ginger Cat opening one eye.

"Quite impossible!" squeaked Grey Rat.

"Quite, quite impossible!" grunted Pink Pig.

"Very well," said Little Red Hen, "I will carry it myself."

And she did. She carried it all the way to the mill. The great stones at the mill turned round and round, grinding the grains into flour. When the flour was fine enough, the miller put it into a linen bag.

"Thank you," said Little Red Hen.

When she came back to the farmyard, Little Red Hen called out,

"Here is the flour . . . Who will help me take it to the baker to be made into bread?"

"Out of the question," said Ginger Cat, walking away.

"Quite out of the question," squeaked Grey Rat, running off.

"Quite, quite out of the question," grunted Pink Pig. "I am too fat to go anywhere."

"I suppose 'out of the question' means 'No'," said Little Red Hen. "I will take it myself."

And she did. She went to the baker and brought back a crusty loaf.

"Who will help me eat this lovely new bread?" she clucked.

The animals all gathered around.

"I will!" said Ginger Cat, twitching his whiskers.

"So will I!" squeaked Grey Rat. "I am so hungry."

"Don't forget me!" grunted Pink Pig. "It looks delicious!"

"It is delicious," said Little Red Hen, "but you didn't help me at all . . . so it is quite out of the question for you to have any of it! Cluck! Cluck!"

Sleeping Beauty

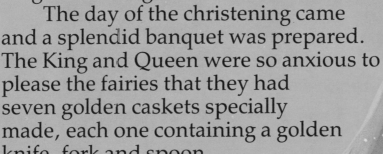

There was once a King and a Queen who longed for a child. After many years of waiting they at last had a daughter. Now at that time, any child who had a fairy as godmother was especially lucky. At the christening the fairy always gave the child a special gift. The King and Queen loved their little daughter so much they invited all seven fairies who lived in their kingdom to be godmothers.

The day of the christening came and a splendid banquet was prepared. The King and Queen were so anxious to please the fairies that they had seven golden caskets specially made, each one containing a golden knife, fork and spoon.

And then, something rather awful happened. As the King and his guests were taking their places at the banqueting table, an old fairy, whom no one had seen for years and years, arrived unexpectedly. The King immediately ordered another place to be set at the table, but alas, there were eight fairies and only seven golden caskets, and the old fairy had to eat with a silver knife, fork and spoon.

The old fairy was very angry. First she hadn't received an invitation and now she wasn't to have a golden casket. She thought she had been slighted on purpose, which wasn't the case at all, and she vowed she would have her revenge.

The time came for the fairies to bestow their gifts upon the baby Princess.

"She shall be as beautiful as a rose," said the first.

"She shall have the nature of an angel," said the second.

"She shall have the grace of a swan," said the third.

"She shall dance to perfection," said the fourth.

"She shall sing like a nightingale," said the fifth.

"She shall play the sweetest music," said the sixth.

No one could find the seventh fairy.

"She shall prick her finger on a spindle . . . and DIE!" cackled the old fairy.

Everyone present gasped, and turned pale. But before anyone could think what to say, or do, the seventh fairy reappeared. She had heard the old fairy mumbling and knew she was up to no good. She had waited until last to bestow her gift so that she could undo any harm done by the old fairy.

"The Princess will prick her finger . . ." she said, "But she will not die. Instead, she will sleep for a hundred years, and be woken by a prince."

The King was taking no chances. He ordered that all the spindles in his kingdom be destroyed. If there was no spindle for the Princess to prick her finger on, then there would be less reason to worry.

Sixteen years passed, and the Princess grew more and more beautiful. Then one day, when the King and Queen were away, she found an old tower. In the room at the very top she found an old woman spinning.

"What are you doing?" asked the Princess. She had never seen a spinning wheel before.

"I am spinning," said the old woman, who for some reason had never heard the King's order regarding spindles.

"May I try?" asked the Princess, and because neither she or the old woman had heard of the fairy's curse, she took the spindle when the old woman handed it to her. Alas, everything came about as the fairy had predicted. The Princess pricked her finger and fell into a swoon from which she did not wake.

There was so much wailing and moaning in the castle that the seventh fairy heard it. Now that the Princess was asleep there was something else she had to do.

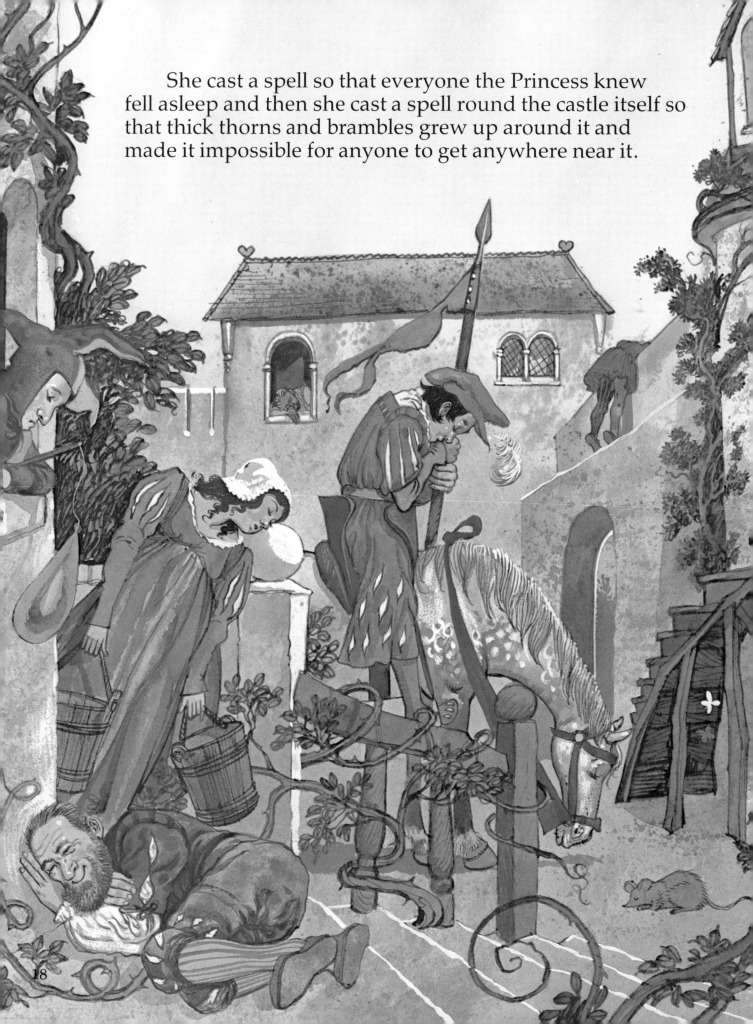

She cast a spell so that everyone the Princess knew fell asleep and then she cast a spell round the castle itself so that thick thorns and brambles grew up around it and made it impossible for anyone to get anywhere near it.

A hundred years passed and many strange stories were told
about the castle. Many tried to get into it, but no one succeeded. And
then one day a King's son happened to pass that way. He asked
about the castle and an old woodcutter told him a story he had
heard from his own father about a princess and a magic spell.

The Prince was curious and decided to look for himself. He unbuckled his sword and prepared to hack through the thorns, but before he could touch them they seemed to melt away, and a path appeared which led to the castle gate.

The castle was very still. There wasn't a sound to be heard anywhere. He found the Princess on the couch where she had been gently laid a hundred years before. She looked so beautiful that he bent to kiss her.

And that was how the seventh fairy's prediction came true. The Prince's kiss woke the Princess, just as the fairy had said it would. And as the Princess woke, so everyone else in the castle woke, and life went on exactly from the point at which it had stopped a hundred years ago. It was as if nothing out of the ordinary had happened at all.

The Prince married the Sleeping Beauty who was now wide awake, and they lived happily ever after.

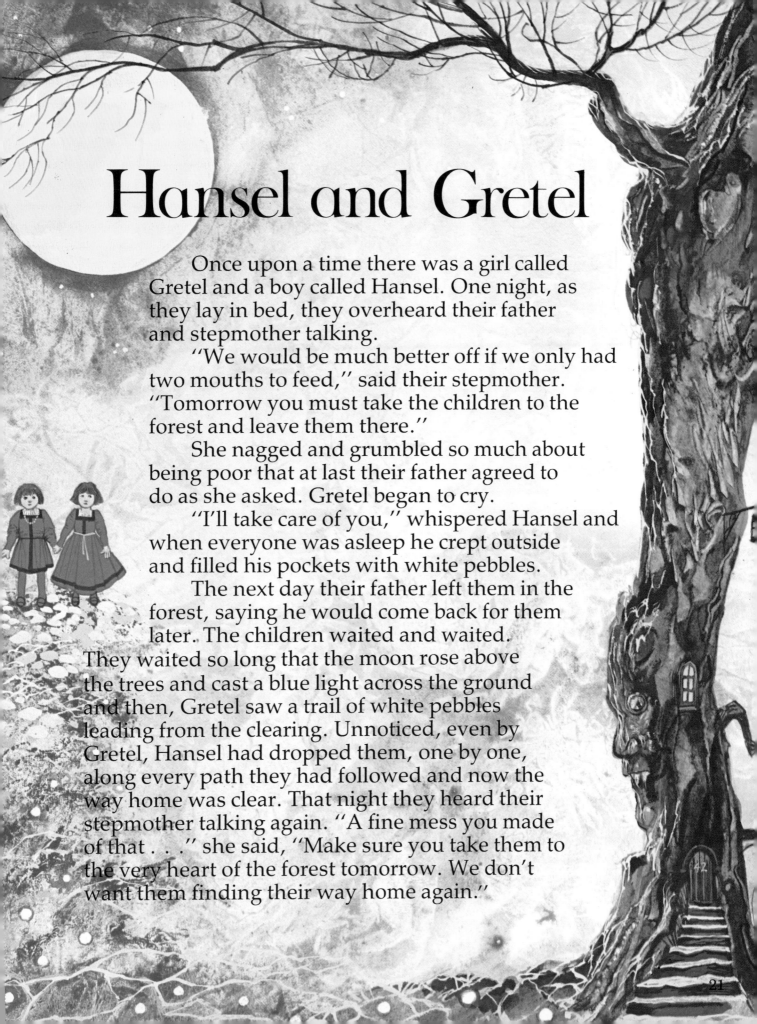

Hansel and Gretel

Once upon a time there was a girl called Gretel and a boy called Hansel. One night, as they lay in bed, they overheard their father and stepmother talking.

"We would be much better off if we only had two mouths to feed," said their stepmother. "Tomorrow you must take the children to the forest and leave them there."

She nagged and grumbled so much about being poor that at last their father agreed to do as she asked. Gretel began to cry.

"I'll take care of you," whispered Hansel and when everyone was asleep he crept outside and filled his pockets with white pebbles.

The next day their father left them in the forest, saying he would come back for them later. The children waited and waited. They waited so long that the moon rose above the trees and cast a blue light across the ground and then, Gretel saw a trail of white pebbles leading from the clearing. Unnoticed, even by Gretel, Hansel had dropped them, one by one, along every path they had followed and now the way home was clear. That night they heard their stepmother talking again. "A fine mess you made of that . . ." she said, "Make sure you take them to the very heart of the forest tomorrow. We don't want them finding their way home again."

"I'll gather some more pebbles," whispered Hansel, but when he went to fill his pockets he found the door of the cottage locked and bolted.

The next day everything happened as it had done before, except that this time, instead of pebbles, Hansel left a trail of white bread crumbs.

Alas, when the moon rose and the children looked eagerly for the crumbs to shine in the moonlight and show them the way home, they discovered there were no crumbs. The birds had eaten them. Now they were really lost.

They had been in the forest three days when they came upon a very strange house. Its walls were made of gingerbread. Its roof was covered with biscuit tiles. Its windows were made of clear see-through toffee. The old woman who lived there invited them inside.

"How kind you are," said Gretel.

"How horrid she is," gasped Gretel when the witch, for the woman was a witch, pushed Hansel into a cage and locked him in.

"Hee . . . hee . . ." said the witch, "Now little girl, you can feed your brother until he is fat enough to eat."

Every day the witch made Hansel eat pies and cakes and custard. She gave Gretel nothing but crusts and gravy.

"Don't worry," whispered Hansel. "I won't let her eat me." And every day, when the witch ordered him to put out his finger so that she could see how fat he was getting, he pushed a stick through the bars instead. The witch couldn't understand why he stayed so thin and bony. Then one morning she said crossly,

"Get the oven ready girl . . . I'm tired of waiting."

Poor Gretel. The tears rolled down her cheeks as the witch made her stoke up the fire.

The oven got hotter and hotter. Poor, poor Hansel. What could she do to save him?

But it wasn't Hansel the witch had decided to cook. It was Gretel herself.

"Climb into the oven and test the temperature," she cackled.

Hansel whispered a warning and Gretel realised just in time what the witch was about to do. The witch didn't get a chance to push her, Gretel pushed the witch instead.

"Let me out!" screamed the witch as Gretel slammed the oven door shut.

Gretel pretended not to hear. She let Hansel out of the cage and they ran into the wood without a backward glance.

They found a path which led them home. Their father was overjoyed to see them and they were overjoyed when he told them that their stepmother had gone. And so, once again, the three of them lived happily together.

Chicken Licken

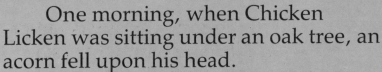

One morning, when Chicken Licken was sitting under an oak tree, an acorn fell upon his head.

"Oh dear," he gasped, "The sky is falling. I must run and tell the King."

On the way to the palace he met his friend Henny Penny.

"Where are you going?" asked Henny Penny.

"To tell the King the sky is falling," said Chicken Licken.

"Then I'll come with you," clucked Henny Penny.

Cocky Locky was scratching for grain.

"Where are you both going in such a hurry?" he asked.

"To tell the King the sky is falling," said Chicken Licken.

"Then I'll come with you," crowed Cocky Locky.

"Where are you all going?" asked Ducky Lucky, when she met them hurrying along a footpath.

"To tell the King the sky is falling," said Chicken Licken without stopping.

"Then I'll come with you," quacked Ducky Lucky.

"Where are you all going?" called Drakey Lakey from the pond.

"To tell the King the sky is falling," said Chicken Licken.

"Then I'll come with you," said Drakey Lakey shaking the water from his webbed feet.

Goosey Loosey was as anxious as everyone else to help tell the King the bad news.

"I'll come with you," she hissed as she stretched her long white neck.

"And I'll come too . . . too . . . too . . ." gobbled Turkey Lurkey who didn't like to be left out of anything.

Foxy Loxy was lurking behind a bush.

"Where are you all going in such a hurry?" he asked slyly.

"To tell the King the sky is falling," said Chicken Licken.

"Then you had better follow me," said Foxy Loxy. "I know of a short cut."

And he led Chicken Licken, Henny Penny, Cocky Locky, Ducky Lucky, Drakey Lakey, Goosey Loosey and Turkey Lurkey through the bushes to his den, where his wife and five hungry children were waiting.

And that, I am sorry to say, was the end of Chicken Licken, Henny Penny, Cocky Locky, Ducky Lucky, Drakey Lakey, Goosey Loosey and Turkey Lurkey, for the fox family had them for dinner, and the King never did find out that a piece of sky had fallen on Chicken Licken's head.

Twelve Dancing Princesses

Once upon a time, there was a King who had twelve beautiful daughters, and an unusual problem. Every night, when the twelve princesses were sent to bed their shoes were perfectly sound. Every morning when they came down to breakfast their shoes were full of holes. Every day the King had to buy twelve pairs of new shoes. That was expensive, though the expense did not worry the King. What did worry him was not knowing WHY the shoes were full of holes.

He tried locking the bedroom door on the outside when all the princesses were safely inside, and sleeping with the key under his pillow. It made no difference. The princesses' shoes were still full of holes in the morning.

The King was so puzzled, and so vexed, because he couldn't find out WHY it was happening that he issued a proclamation.

It said, WHOMSOEVER SHALL DISCOVER WHY THE PRINCESSES' SHOES ARE FULL OF HOLES EVERY MORNING SHALL HAVE ONE OF THE PRINCESSES FOR HIS WIFE AND SHALL INHERIT MY KINGDOM WHEN I DIE.

Princes came from far and wide to try to find an answer to the mystery. Not one of them succeeded. The puzzled King was beginning to despair of ever finding an answer when a poor soldier came to the palace. The proclamation had said nothing about being a prince if you wanted to solve the mystery, so he had decided to make an attempt at it himself.

The King received the soldier as kindly, and as grandly, as any of the Princes, and that night he was taken to a room adjoining the princesses' bedroom so that he could keep watch.

Now it so happened, that the soldier had been kind to a wise old woman on his way to the palace, and she had given him a cloak, and some advice. "When the princesses offer you wine," she had said, "pretend to drink it and then pretend to fall asleep. Wear the cloak when you want to be invisible."

That night, when the princesses were ready for bed, the eldest said to the soldier,

'You must be thirsty. Take this cup of wine and drink."

The soldier remembered the wise woman's words and pretended to drink. And then, he pretended to get drowsy. Presently he closed his eyes as though he was asleep.

As soon as they heard him snore the princesses jumped from their beds and put on their shoes and their prettiest dresses.

"Are you all ready?" asked the eldest.

"We are ready," replied her sisters.

The eldest princess pressed a carved leaf on the end of her bed. The bed moved slowly to one side and revealed a hidden staircase leading down into the earth. The princesses picked up their skirts and hurried down the steps, the eldest leading the way, and the youngest following last of all.

The soldier, who of course was awake and had seen everything, put the cloak the old woman had given him round his shoulders. It covered him from head to toe and made him completely invisible.

He ran after the princesses and caught up with them at the bottom of the steps. He was in such a hurry not to be left behind that he accidentally stepped on the hem of the youngest princess's dress, and tore it.

"Oh . . ." she gasped. "Someone has stepped on my dress."

"Don't be silly," said her sisters. "You caught it on a nail . . . come hurry . . . we must not be late."

At the bottom of the steps there was a wood in which all the trees had silver leaves. The soldier broke off one, and put it in his pocket.

"What was that?" cried the youngest princess in alarm, as she heard the snap of the breaking twig.

"It was nothing . . ." said her sisters.

Next, they passed through an avenue in which all the trees had golden leaves. Again the princess heard the snap of a breaking twig, but again her sisters told her it was her own imagination playing tricks on her.

The running princesses came to the shores of a wide blue lake. At the edge of the lake were twelve boats, with twelve handsome princes sitting, waiting, at the oars. The soldier sat in the boat which was to carry the youngest princess.

"I wonder what makes the boat so heavy today," said the prince, as he pulled, harder than usual, at the oars.

On the far side of the lake there was a magnificent palace from which the sounds of music and merry-making came . . . and it was there that the mystery of the worn out shoes was solved. The twelve princesses danced the entire night with the twelve handsome princes.

Just before dawn, and when all their shoes were in shreds, the princes rowed the princesses back across the lake, and the princesses ran home.

As soon as they reached their bedroom they hurried to look at the soldier. He had run home ahead of them and they found him on his bed, still sleeping, or so they thought.

"We are safe . . ." said the eldest princess.

The soldier followed the princesses to the secret palace the next night, and the following night too. On the third night he took the jewelled cup from which the youngest princess drank and slipped it into a pocket in the invisible cloak.

On the morning after the third night, the King sent for the soldier, and said,

"Your time is up. Either tell me why my daughters' shoes are worn through every morning, or be banished forever . . ."

"Your daughters' shoes are worn because they dance every night in an underground palace," said the soldier, and he told the King all that he had seen.

The princesses gasped and turned pale as the soldier took the silver leaf, the golden leaf, and the jewelled cup from his pocket and handed them to the King. They knew now they could not deny that what the soldier said was true.

"We must confess," said the eldest princess.

The King was so relieved to have the mystery of the worn shoes explained, he couldn't stay cross with his daughters for long.

"Now I shall be able to sleep at night," he said.

The King kept the promise he had made in the proclamation, and the soldier married the princess of his choice. And many years later, when the old King died, he became King in his place.

The Princess

Once there was a prince who wanted to marry a Princess. He travelled far and wide, for many months, searching for one. He met many girls who said they were Princesses, but somehow he could never be quite sure they were telling him the truth.

It was a very sad Prince who returned alone to the palace.

One dark night, not long after his return, there was a dreadful storm. It rained, and it thundered, and bright flashes of lightning lit up the sky. Everyone was saying how glad he was not to be outside, when there was a knock at the palace door. The King himself went to answer it.

A wet bedraggled girl stood shivering on the doorstep. "Come in, come in at once," he cried, "You must shelter here for the night."

When the girl was dry and warm again, and had eaten supper, she told them that she was a Princess. The Prince wished he could believe her, for of all the girls who said they were Princesses, this was the one he most wanted to believe.

Now the Prince's mother was very wise, and that night, without telling anyone what she was doing she re-made the girl's bed. She put one tiny pea on the smooth wooden bed . . . and on top of the pea she put twenty soft mattresses . . . and on top of the mattresses, she put twenty, very soft, feather pillows. The girl had to climb almost to the ceiling before she could get into it!

Next morning the Queen asked her how well she had slept.

"I hardly slept at all," sighed the girl. "The bed was so lumpy, I tossed and turned and twisted all night."

As soon as she heard that, the Queen took the girl by the hand and led her to the Prince.

and the Pea

"Only a real Princess could lie on so many soft mattresses and be unable to sleep because of one tiny pea," she said. And she explained to everyone what she had done.

The Prince was overjoyed, and he and the Princess were married, and of course they lived happily ever after. Princes and Princesses always do.

The Three Little Pigs

Once upon a time there were three little pigs who lived together in one house. As they grew bigger their house seemed to grow smaller, and one day they decided to build three separate houses.

The first little pig built himself a house of straw.

The second little pig built himself a house of sticks.

The third little pig built himself a house of bricks.

The house of bricks took much longer to build than the other two, but it was the strongest when it was finished.

Soon after the first little pig had moved into his house there was a knock at the door.

"Little pig, little pig let me come in," said the wily old wolf, thinking how nice it would be to have pig for dinner.

"No, no, by the hair of my chinny chin chin, I will not let you in," said the first little pig.

"Then I'll huff, and I'll puff, and I'll blow your house in," growled the wolf.

And that is exactly what he did. The straw house blew

away in the wind and the wolf gobbled up the pig.

When the wolf saw the house built of sticks, he licked his lips and said:

"Little pig, little pig, let me come in."

"No, no, by the hair of my chinny chin chin, I will not let you in," said the second little pig.

"Then I'll huff, and I'll puff, and I'll blow your house in," growled the wolf.

The house of sticks was as easy to blow down as the house of straw, and that was the end of the second little pig.

The wolf knew there was a third little pig about somewhere and when he saw the house of bricks he called through the letter box.

"Let me in little pig."

"No, no, by the hair of my chinny chin chin, I will not let you in," said the third little pig.

"Then I'll huff and I'll puff and I'll blow your house in," said the wolf.

And the wolf huffed and he

puffed, and he puffed and he huffed, until he was quite out of breath, and still the house of bricks stood firm and secure. It didn't even creak.

"I can see I'll have to be rather clever to catch this little pig," said the wolf. "I'll have to lure him outside his house."

He told the little pig about a field he knew where the turnips were ready for digging, and arranged to meet him there next morning.

But the third little pig was

much cleverer than the wolf realised. He knew exactly what the wolf was up to. He had been to the field, dug up the turnips and was safely back indoors before the wolf had even woken up.

The wolf tried to keep his temper. He told the little pig about a tree he knew that was weighed down with juicy red apples.

"I'll meet you there in the morning," he said slyly.

The wolf wasn't going to be caught again and next day he

got up very early. When he reached the orchard the little pig was still in the tree picking apples.

"I'll throw you one," called the little pig, and he threw an apple so that it rolled into the long grass.

While the wolf was looking for it the little pig jumped from the tree and ran home. He was safely inside his brick house before the wolf realised he had been tricked.

By this time the wolf was getting very annoyed . . .

and hungry.

"I'll meet you at the fair tomorrow," he said.

The little pig did go to the fair next day. He bought himself a butter churn. He was on his way home when he caught sight of the wolf. As quick as a raindrop hiding in a puddle, he hid himself in the butter churn and began to roll down the hill. He rolled right over the wolf's foot and frightened him horribly. He was safely inside his brick house before the wolf stopped trembling.

When the wolf discovered who had been inside the butter churn he was very angry indeed. He was determined that the little pig should not escape again. He climbed on to the roof of the brick house and began to ease himself down the brick chimney.

The little pig was very frightened when he heard the wolf mumbling and grumbling inside his chimney, but he didn't panic. He built up the fire and set his biggest cooking pot on the flames.

The wolf slithered down the chimney and fell into the pot with an enormous splash and a very loud OUCH!!! And that, I am glad to say, was the end of the wolf.

Little Red Riding Hood

Red Riding Hood lived with her mother in a little cottage on the edge of a wood. Her grandmother lived on the other side of the wood.

One day her mother gave Red Riding Hood a basket of nice things to eat, butter, honey and new-laid eggs.

"Take these to Grandma," said her mother. "She is not well. Keep to the path now. Give Grandma my love and then come home."

"I will," said Red Riding Hood. She waved goodbye.

It was a lovely sunny morning. Red Riding Hood was humming to herself as she came to the wood. She looked very pretty in her red hood and cloak. The birds peeped through the leaves to see her pass. The robin even sang a song for her. A squirrel at the top of a tree, stopped nibbling a nut – just to watch her.

41

When Red Riding Hood came to the middle of the wood, she stopped to pick some flowers. A wolf came along the path to meet her.

"Good morning, my dear," he said. "Where are you going?"

"I am going to see my Grandma," said Red Riding Hood. "She is not well."

"Oh dear," said the wolf kindly, "I am sorry. Have you far to go?"

"Just to the cottage at the end of this path," said Red Riding Hood.

"Well," said the wolf, "I'll say good-day; I am going down this way. I hope your Grandma feels better soon . . . Goodbye!"

Red Riding Hood went on her way, but the wolf did not keep to his path. He turned round and ran along another one to get to Grandma's cottage first.

Grandma saw him coming, and hid under her bed. Her nightcap fell onto the floor.

In came the wolf. He put the nightcap on and climbed into bed.

When Red Riding Hood came to the cottage door, she lifted the latch and walked in. She went over to her Grandma's bed and sat down.

"Look, Grandma, I've brought you lots of nice things to eat . . . Shall I put them in the cupboard?" There was no answer.

When Red Riding Hood turned towards Grandma again, two staring eyes, under a nightcap, watched her from the pillow. The frilly nightcap had slipped and she could see one large ear. 'How Grandma has changed,' thought Red Riding Hood.

"Oh, Grandma," she whispered, "what big ears you have!"

"All the better to hear you with, my dear," said the wolf. How strange Grandma sounded.

"Oh, Grandma, what big eyes you have!"

"All the better to see you with, my dear," said the wolf with a smile.

"Oh, Grandma," said Red Riding Hood, "what big teeth you have!"

"All the better to EAT you with!" said the wolf. He leapt out of the bed, and tried to catch her.

Red Riding Hood screamed. She ran as fast as she could out of the house and down the path into the wood.

Two woodcutters were busy cutting down trees. They heard Red Riding Hood calling for help. At once, they left their work and chased the wolf.

How he ran when he saw the men coming after him! How funny he looked with Grandma's frilly nightcap flapping up and down on one ear! They all watched until the wolf had gone. He was never seen again.

Red Riding Hood was so glad.

"Will you help me to find my Grandma, please?" she asked her woodcutter friends.

"Of course we will," they said. Then hand in hand, they all went back to Grandma's cottage.

They looked everywhere for Grandma, but could not find her. They were not looking in the right place, were they?

"Grandma!" called Red Riding Hood. "Where are you? . . ."

"I am here!" said a small voice, and then came a big sneeze. "A . . . TISHOO!"

The frill round the bottom of the bed shook. Red Riding Hood lifted it up to peep underneath. There was Grandma, safe and sound.

"Oh, Grandma!" she cried. "How clever you are!"

When Grandma was back in her bed, Red Riding Hood found her a clean nightcap. They were very happy – all laughing and talking together.

"I feel better," said Grandma. "Let's have a party!"

And they did . . . Lovely brown eggs, with fresh bread and butter, and golden honey.

One woodcutter went to fetch Red Riding Hood's mother. They all had a happy time. The squirrel sprang from branch to branch and all the birds sang louder and louder.

Puss in Boots

Once upon a time, there was a miller, who had three sons. When he died he left his mill to his first son, his donkey to his second son, and because he had nothing else, he left his cat to his third son.

The first son ground flour at the mill and sold it. The second son harnessed the donkey to a cart and carried things for paying customers. But what could the third son do with a cat, except let him sit in the sun, and purr, and drink milk?

One day, the cat said, "Master, give me a pair of boots and a sack and you will see that I am not as useless as you think." It was a very strange request for a cat to make, but it was granted nonetheless.

The cat, or Puss in Boots, as the miller's son now called him, went into the forest and caught a rabbit. He put it in the sack and then instead of taking it home to the miller's son, he took it to the King's palace.

"Please accept this small present from my master the Marquis of Carabas," said Puss in Boots.

It was to be the first of many presents Puss in Boots took to the King, and each time he said he had been sent by his master the Marquis of Carabas. And though the King never actually met the Marquis of Carabas, he soon became very familiar with his name. The miller's son knew nothing of the presents, or of the Marquis of Carabas, and Puss in Boots didn't tell him.

One day, when Puss in Boots was at the palace, he overheard someone say that the King was about to take his daughter for a drive in the country. Puss in Boots hurried home.

"Quick master!" he called. "Go and bathe in the river and I will make your fortune."

It was another strange request for a cat to make but the miller's son was used to his pet by now and so he did as he was told. No sooner was he in the river than Puss in Boots took his clothes and threw them into the river with him.

"Puss . . . Puss . . . what are you doing?" called the miller's son.

Puss didn't answer, he was watching the road. Presently he saw the King's carriage in the distance. He waited until it was close then he ran out in the road in front of it.

"Help! Help! My master the Marquis of Carabas is drowning! Please save him!"

It took but a moment to drag the miller's son, who hadn't the slightest idea what Puss in Boots was up to, from the river and find him some dry clothes. He looked so handsome in the fine velvet tunic and the doublet and hose borrowed from one of the footmen that the princess fell in love with him at once.

"Father dear, may the Marquis of Carabas ride with us?"

The King liked to please his daughter and agreed to her request at once.

"Will you ride with us Puss?" asked the King.

Puss asked to be excused. He said he had something rather important to attend to. He ran on ahead of the carriage, and each time he saw someone at work in the fields he called,

"If the King asks who this land belongs to, tell him it belongs to the Marquis of Carabas."

The King did stop the carriage several times, and each time he received the same answer to his question.

'The Marquis of Carabas must be a very rich man,' he thought.

Puss in Boots ran so swiftly that soon he was a long way ahead of the carriage. Presently he came to a rich and imposing looking castle, which he knew belonged to a cruel and wicked ogre. He went straight up to the ogre without so much as a twitching of a whisker, and said,

"I hear you can turn yourself into any animal you choose. I won't believe a story like that unless I see it for myself."

Immediately, the ogre changed himself into a lion, and roared and growled and snarled.

"There . . ." he said, when he had turned himself back into an ogre. "I hope I frightened you."

"Must be easy to change yourself into something big," said Puss in Boots with a shrug. "I don't suppose you can turn yourself into something as small as a . . . er . . . um . . ." He seemed to be thinking. ". . . er . . . um . . . a mouse?"

The ogre couldn't have a mere cat doubting his special abilities. He changed himself into a tiny mouse in the twinkling of an eye. It was the last time he changed himself into anything because Puss in Boots pounced on him and ate him up before he could change back into an ogre, and THAT was the end of him!

"Hoorah!" shouted the castle servants. "We are free of the wicked ogre at last. Hoorah!"

"Your new master will always be kind, you can be sure of that," said Puss in Boots.

"Who IS our new master?" they asked.

"The Marquis of Carabas of course," said Puss.

When the King's carriage reached the castle, Puss in Boots was standing at the drawbridge, with the smiling servants gathered round him.

"Welcome. ." he said with a beautiful bow. "Welcome to the home of my master the Marquis of Carabas." The miller's son was too astonished to do anything except think to himself,

'Whatever is Puss up to?'

Luckily Puss had time to explain while the King was getting out of the carriage.

'What a rich man this Marquis must be,' thought the King. 'And such a nice young man too.'

Not long afterwards the princess and the miller's son were married. They, and Puss in Boots, lived happily ever after in the castle that had once belonged to the wicked ogre.

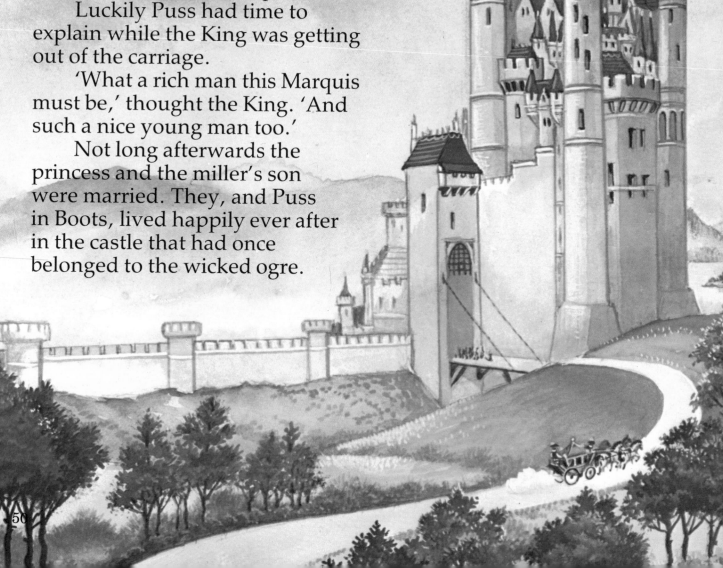

The Ugly Duckling

Once, somewhere in the country, there was a duck who had a clutch of eggs to hatch. Five of them hatched into fluffy little ducklings, but the sixth, which for some reason was bigger than all the others, lay in the nest, smooth and unbroken.

"Thats much too big to be a duck egg," said one of the duck's friends. "Looks more like a turkey egg to me."

"How will I be able to tell?" asked the duck.

"It will not swim when it is hatched," said her friend. "Turkeys never do."

But the egg wasn't a turkey egg because the bird that hatched from it DID swim. It swam as well as any duckling.

"That last duckling of yours is very ugly," laughed the farmyard hens. It was true. He wasn't a bit like his brothers and sisters.

"What an ugly duckling," laughed the geese when they saw him. And somehow that name stuck. Whenever anyone wanted him they called, "Ugly duckling, where are you?" or if they didn't want him they said "Ugly duckling go away." He even thought of himself as ugly duckling. He was very sad. He didn't like being ugly. He didn't like being teased. No one would play with him. No one would swim with him. Even his mother made fun of him. One day, the ugly duckling ran away. And I am sorry to say, no one missed him at all.

The ugly duckling hoped he would find someone in the big wide world, to be his friend. Someone who wouldn't mind how ugly he was. But the wild ducks were just as unkind as the farmyard ducks, and the wild geese honked at him and made fun, just as the farmyard geese had done.

"Am I never to find a friend? Am I never to be happy?" sighed the ugly duckling.

One day, as he sat alone and unhappy in the middle of a lake on the bleak flat marshes, he heard the steady beat of wings. When he looked up there were swans flying overhead with their long necks stretched before them and their white feathers gleaming in the sun. They were so beautiful. If only he had been born a swan. But he hadn't. He had been born a duckling and an ugly one at that.

The ugly duckling stayed on the lake
all through the long hard winter. Food
was hard to find and he was often hungry.
Once he was trapped in some ice and
thought he would die. He was set free,
just in time, by a farmer and his dog.

Spring came and the lake where he had
spent the lonely winter became a busy,
exciting, and noisy place. The ducks
were forever quacking and the geese were
forever honking. There was plenty of
splashing and excitement. But not for
the ugly duckling. No one quacked the
latest piece of gossip to him. Sadly he
spread his wings and took to the sky.
He had never flown before and he was
surprised how strong his wings were.
They carried him away from the lake and
the marshes and over a leafy garden.

On a still, clear pond in the garden,
he could see the beautiful white swans,
with their gracefully arched necks, and
suddenly the ugly duckling felt that he
did not want to live any longer.

"I will go down to the pond and ask
those beautiful birds to kill me," he
said. And down he went to the water.
He bent his head humbly and closed his
eyes.

"Kill me," he said to the swans. "I am too ugly to live."

"Ugly?" said the swans. "Have you looked at your reflection?"

"I do not need to look. I know how ugly I am," said the ugly duckling.

"Look into the water." said the swans. And so the ugly duckling did. What he saw made his heart beat fast and filled him with happiness. During the long winter months he had changed.

"I'm . . . I'm just like you . . ." he whispered.

When the children who lived in the garden came to feed the swans they called to one another,

"A new swan . . . a new swan . . . isn't he beautiful?" And then the ugly duckling knew without a doubt that he really WAS a swan, that he had ALWAYS been a swan and that his days of being lonely were over.

Rumpelstiltskin

Once there was a miller who had a beautiful daughter. He was always talking about her and saying how clever she was.

One day, the miller had to take some flour to the palace. He told the king about his daughter.

"Her hair is like spun gold, Your Majesty, and what is more, she is so clever she can spin straw into gold."

This was not true. The miller's daughter had never even spun cloth but the king did not know this.

"Bring your daughter to me!" said the king.

The miller almost danced down the steps of the palace. He took his daughter to see the king the very next day.

The king led her into a room where there was a pile of straw, a stool and a spinning wheel.

"Now," said the king. "You must spin this straw into gold by dawn tomorrow or you shall die."

He left the room and locked the door.

The miller's daughter could not understand. How could she spin straw into gold? How could she spin anything? She did not even know how to begin. She crept into a corner of the room and burst into tears.

Suddenly, there was a puff of smoke and a strange little man stood beside her. His face was brown and wrinkled, his nose was long and his white beard almost reached his knobbly knees.

"What's the matter?" he said. "Why are you crying?"

"Whatever shall I do?" the girl said tearfully. "Look at all this straw! The king has said I must spin it into gold by early morning or I shall die! I cannot even spin!"

"Dry your tears," said the little man. "What will you give me if I spin it for you?"

The girl's fingers touched the necklace she was wearing.

"I will give you my necklace," she said.

The strange little man clapped his hands with delight. He sat down to spin. The spinning wheel whirled around. It made a gentle humming sound. The girl's eyes closed and she fell asleep.

While she slept, the straw became a pile of gold. She awoke; the strange little man had vanished.

In the morning, the king could not believe his eyes. A heap of shining gold! "Come with me," he said at once. The king led the girl into a much larger room, which was filled with even more straw. He told her she must spin it into gold by the next day.

Once again the door was locked and the poor girl began to cry. Once more there was a puff of smoke and there stood the strange little man.

"What will you give me this time if I spin the straw?" he asked.

"Oh, thank you, thank you," she said. "I will give you the ring my mother gave me." She slipped the ring off her finger and held it out to him. Without another word, he took it and started to spin.

The next day, although the king was delighted with the gold, he was not satisfied. He took the miller's daughter into a larger room with heaps of straw which nearly reached the ceiling.

"Now, my dear," he said. "Spin all this straw into gold tonight and I will make you my queen."

This time, the girl was very frightened. She knew that if the little man appeared, she had nothing left to give him.

Once again there was a puff of smoke and there he stood. As if he knew already, the strange little man said,

"Promise me that when you are queen, you will give me your first baby. If you promise, I will spin the straw for you."

'How can I promise?' she thought. 'I may never be queen . . . or have a child . . . but it's the only way to get the spinning done.'

"I promise," she whispered.

The strange little man spun the straw into gold and vanished as before.

Next day, the king kept his word. He married the miller's daughter and she became queen.

Some years later, the queen sat smiling at her first baby.
A voice behind her said,
    "Remember your promise? I have come for the child." It
was the strange little man.
    "Oh, no! Do not make me give you my baby!" she begged.
"Take all my other treasure, but let me keep him! Please,
please!"
    "I will give you one chance," he said. "You have three
days in which to tell me my name. If you find my right name,
you may keep the child."

The queen wrote down every name she could think of and sent her servants out to find new names.

"Is it William? . . . David? . . . Rupert?" she asked, when the little man came the next day. To each one he replied, "That is not my name."

On the second day, she tried funny names like Cross-Patch, Double-Dutch and Hanky-Panky, but still he replied,

"That is not my name."

On the third morning, a servant rushed in to see the queen.

"Your Majesty!" he said, "I was in the forest . . . there was a little hut with a fire outside. A strange little man was hopping round it and singing!"

"What was he singing?" asked the queen.

"He sang something like this, Your Majesty . . .

'I will dance and I will sing
Tomorrow will the baby bring
The queen she cannot spoil my game
For Rumpelstiltskin is my name!'

The queen was so happy when she heard this. She gave the servant a bag of gold.

When the strange little man came, he asked,

"Well, my lady, what is my name?"

"James, perhaps?" said the queen. "Richard?"

"No, no," replied the strange little man.

"Rumpelstiltskin then?" said the queen slowly.

The strange little man howled with rage and stamped so hard that his foot sank right through the floor.

"Who told you my name? A witch? Yes, a witch!" he shouted. With a great puff of smoke and in a flash the strange little man was gone. No one ever saw him again.